Star Stories

To Dad, forever my guiding star—A.W.

To Jovan and Kiran, two shining stars—A.G.

Running Press Kids
Hachette Book Group
1290 Avenue of the Americas, New York, NY 10104
www.runningpress.com/rpkids
@RP_Kids

Printed in China

Originally published in 2018 by Templar Publishing
in the United Kingdom.
First U.S. Edition: July 2019

Published by Running Press Kids, an imprint of Perseus
Books, LLC, a subsidiary of Hachette Book Group, Inc.
The Running Press Kids name and logo is a trademark of
the Hachette Book Group.

The Hachette Speakers Bureau provides a wide range of
authors for speaking events. To find out more, go to www.
hachettespeakersbureau.com or call (866) 376-6591.

The publisher is not responsible for websites (or their
content) that are not owned by the publisher.

Print book cover and interior design by Olivia Cook.

Library of Congress Control Number: 2018948409

ISBNs: 978-0-7624-9505-4 (hardcover),
978-0-7624-9504-7 (ebook)

TLF

10 9 8 7 6 5 4 3

Star
Stories

Illustrated by Andy Wilx

Written by Anita Ganeri

RP|KIDS
PHILADELPHIA

Contents

(Name of Story—Inspiration)

Ancient Greece

Phaeton and the Swan—Cygnus 7

The White-Winged Horse—Pegasus 10

The Golden Fleece—Aries 14

The Dog and the Fox—Canis Major and Canis Minor 21

Callisto and Arcas—Ursa Major and Ursa Minor 24

The Labors of Heracles—Heracles 27

Andromeda and the Sea Monster—Andromeda 34

North and South America

The Polar Bear and the Three Runners—Nanurjuk (Taurus) 38

Grandmother Spider and the Sun—The Sun 41

How Fisher Brought Summer—The Big Dipper 45

How Coyote Scattered the Stars—The Milky Way 50

The Llama Star—The Milky Way 55

Africa

The Sun God and the Snake—The Sun   57

The Pharaoh's Soul—Orion   61

How Giraffe Became a Star—The Southern Cross   66

Asia

Gilgamesh and the Bull—Taurus   69

The Dog in Heaven—Sirius   75

The Bridge of Magpies—Cygnus and The Milky Way   79

Australia and Oceania

The Canoe of Stars—The Milky Way   83

Hina and the Shark—Orion's Belt   86

The Seven Sisters—Pleiades   89

The Emu Egg and the Sun—The Sun   92

Emu in the Sky—The Milky Way   95

CYGNUS

Phaeton and the Swan

A TALE FROM ANCIENT GREECE

Among the stars of the northern skies is a majestic swan, its long neck and wings outstretched. Long ago, the swan was a man who lived on Earth. Today, it glides through the Milky Way, for all eternity.

At the far end of the Earth, the golden palace of Helios, the Sun god, was a magnificent place. With each new dawn, as the stars faded and the night sky grew pale, Helios burst through the fortress gates and drove his gleaming chariot through the sky, bringing light to the world once more. The chariot was pulled by four fiery horses and was so bright that few could bear its glow.

Day after day, Helios's mortal son, Phaeton, had watched his father race across the heavens. Now, he had a request to make: "Please, Father," he said, "let me drive your chariot. Just for one day."

Shaking his head, Helios turned blazing eyes on his son. "I cannot grant your wish," he said. "The path through the sky is too dangerous for you. At first,

it rises so steeply that my horses can hardly climb. Then, it soars so high that even *my* heart trembles with fear. Finally, it charges down—one false move and you would dive headlong into the sea. Ask me for anything, but not this."

But Phaeton had been waiting for this day for years and, besides, there was no time to lose. The gates of dawn were already peeking open, spreading its rosy glow across the world. So, reluctantly, Helios agreed. The horses were yoked to the chariot, and, taking the reins, Phaeton sped off, dizzy with delight.

Suddenly, disaster struck. The horses were used to a heavier load and, unburdened, they ran wild. From high to low, low to high, the chariot veered, and where it touched the Earth, it set it ablaze. Mountains erupted with fire, rivers and lakes dried up, deserts were scorched, and whole forests burned to the ground. Swept along by the fiery will of the horses, terrified Phaeton called on the gods for help.

The gods knew that they must act quickly if they were to save the Earth. Mighty Zeus seized a thunderbolt and hurled it at the chariot, shattering it into pieces. Wreathed in flames, Phaeton was thrown through the sky until he plummeted to his death in the river far below.

When Cygnus, Phaeton's closest friend, learned of his fate, he searched for many days until he came upon the Sun god's chariot, lying broken and burned. Again and again, Cygnus dived into the water, yet however how hard he tried, he could not swim deep enough to reach Phaeton. Exhausted, and overcome with grief, Cygnus wept for his dead friend. Phaeton's sisters, too, gathered on the riverbank and wept, until eventually they were transformed into poplar trees and their tears turned to golden amber.

Moved by Cygnus's sadness, great Zeus took pity and appeared before him.

"If I transform you into a swan you shall be able to swim more strongly than any man," he said, "but never again will you take human form."

Cygnus paused, imagining living his life forever more as a swan. Then, he remembered his dear friend, and solemnly he agreed. As he stood at the water's edge, his mouth became a rounded beak and white feathers hid his hair. His neck grew long, and his arms became powerful wings, while his feet were now gray and webbed. This time, when he plunged into the raging waters he could swim with ease. And so, swiftly, gently, he retrieved Phaeton's body.

Zeus had been watching from the heavens and was so impressed by Cygnus's sacrifice that he placed him among the stars. There, he flies, still, through the Milky Way, singing his sad swansong in memory of his friend. And, to this day, earthly swans can be found ducking their slender necks beneath the water, while poplar trees grow tall beside the riverbanks.

PEGASUS

The White-Winged Horse

A TALE FROM ANCIENT GREECE

Soaring high among the stars shines Pegasus, the white-winged horse. Ridden by heroes on their daring adventures, he carries thunderbolts for the king of the gods. The rising of his constellation marks the coming of spring and, in Greece, the season of thunderstorms. His story begins long ago, in the kingdom of King Polydectes.

For many years, Perseus lived in Polydectes's palace and was eager to repay the king's hospitality. At a great feast held in the king's honor, Perseus promised to bring him a priceless gift—the head of Medusa. This would be no easy task, even for the greatest of heroes. For Medusa was a hideous monster, with scratching claws of bronze, scaly wings, and fangs like great boar tusks. Worse still, around her head writhed a ring of snakes, flickering and hissing like living flames. Anyone who dared to look at her would instantly be turned to stone.

It was Athena who had transformed Medusa and her two sisters into monsters, and it was Athena who now came to Perseus's aid. Along with magic

winged sandals, a sickle, and a helmet of invisibility, she gave him a gleaming bronze shield, as well as a piece of advice.

"Never look at Medusa directly," she told him, "only at her reflection."

So, Perseus sailed to the farthest edge of the Western Ocean and the entrance to the Underworld. The air was thick with the stench of sulphur, and lava spewed from cavernous cracks in the Earth. All around stood the petrified remains of unwary visitors, frozen still like sinister statues. It was in this dreadful place that Perseus discovered Medusa's lair.

He waited until the sisters were sleeping. Then, hovering above Medusa in his winged sandals, he lifted Athena's shield to catch the monster's reflection and carefully took aim. Lightning fast, he brought down the sickle and cut off Medusa's head. Medusa's sisters sprang up, roaring with fury, but Perseus, wearing his magic helmet, escaped unseen, carrying his gruesome gift. And from the blood of slain Medusa, two magical beings appeared—one a warrior, Chrysaor, golden sword in hand; the other Pegasus, a gleaming white horse, with a mane that flowed like snowfall.

Gliding through the skies on feathered wings, Pegasus never faltered or grew weary. Once, landing high on Mount Helicon, he stamped his hoof on the ground, causing a spring to burst up. From this spring came the nine Muses, goddesses of music and poetry. When the Muses began to sing, the sound that filled the air was so beautiful that the land, sea, and sky all stood still. Even mighty Mount Helicon began to rise into the air until Pegasus brought it back down to Earth with a kick of his heel.

★ ★ ★

For years, the fearsome Chimaera—part-lion, part-goat, part-snake—had terrorized the land of Lycia, snorting great flames that scorched the countryside.

The White-Winged Horse

In despair, the king sent the hero Bellerophon to kill the beast. No one had ever approached the Chimaera and survived to tell the tale but, once again, Athena stepped in to help. In a dream, she appeared to Bellerophon, holding a gleaming golden bridle. When Bellerophon awoke, he found, to his great surprise, that the bridle lay in his hand. He tracked Pegasus down to a mountain stream, slipped the bridle over the horse's head, and leapt on to his back. Then, whisper quiet, Pegasus spread his soft, white wings and rose into the air, parting the clouds with his hooves.

On they flew through the skies to the Chimaera's cave. Pegasus swiftly swooped down on the creature, while Bellerophon plunged his spear into its throat. The Chimaera was dead. To show his gratitude, the King of Lycia showered Bellerophon with honors and gifts, but all was not well. As Bellerophon's fame grew, so did his pride, until he thought of himself as equal to the gods. One day, he put the golden bridle on Pegasus and set off to fly to Mount Olympus, the home of the gods, where no human was allowed. Zeus was furious at Bellerophon and decided to teach him a lesson. He sent a fly that buzzed around Pegasus, biting him and tormenting him, and driving him quite mad. As Pegasus reared up, Bellerophon was thrown from his back, landing down on Earth in a thorn bush and in disgrace.

As for Pegasus, the white-winged horse continued his journey to Olympus where he was taken to live in the heavenly stables of Zeus. As Zeus's bearer of thunderbolts, he served the king of the gods long and loyally. Eventually, to reward Pegasus's faithful service, Zeus turned him into a constellation, one of the largest in the sky. And, on the day he took his place among the stars, legend says, a single, pure-white feather fluttered gently down to Earth.

The Golden Fleece

A TALE FROM ANCIENT GREECE

If you look carefully at the night sky, you may notice three bright stars that make up Aries the ram, with his long curling horns. Centuries ago, people pointed at these stars and told tales of a magical fleece and a great band of heroes who traveled the seas in search of it.

Long ago, King Athamas ruled the kingdom of Boeotia in central Greece, with his wife, Nephele, goddess of the clouds. The couple had two children—Phrixus and his twin sister Helle—but their marriage was not a happy one. Soon, Athamas fell in love with Ino, princess of Thebes, abandoned Nephele, and married Ino instead. Sadly for the doting king, jealous Ino hated her two stepchildren and spent her days devising a plan to be rid of them once and for all.

One night, she ordered her servant to light a fire beneath the grain store. The flames scorched the precious seeds, so that they died as soon as they were

planted, and, across the land, the harvests failed. In despair, people turned to their king for help.

In haste, King Athamas sent a messenger to Delphi to consult the Oracle. There, the god Apollo spoke to mortals through his priestess and told them what they must do. But while Athamas and his people waited anxiously for a reply, growing hungrier by the day, wicked Ino continued her scheming. As the messenger made his way back from Delphi, Ino ambushed him on the road and bribed him to lie about what he had heard. When he finally reached Athamas, he told the king:

"Majesty, you must sacrifice your son to the gods—or the people will starve."

Filled with alarm, Athamas wept bitter tears yet dared not call into question mighty Apollo's advice. Next morning, with a heavy heart, the king led Phrixus to the top of Mount Laphystium, a cloud-capped peak that overlooked the royal palace. Dutifully, Phrixus knelt down and, raising his sword, Athamas offered a final, anguished prayer to the gods.

Yet the sword never reached Phrixus's neck. Unbeknown to the king, Nephele had been keeping watch over her children from the skies above. Just as the blade began to fall, she parted the gathering clouds to reveal a magnificent winged ram, with a fleece of purest gold.

Leaping onto its back, Phrixus called to Helle, his sister, to join him. The golden-robed ram sped eastward, carrying them towards the distant land of Colchis. Their story should have ended happily, but as they flew high above the sea, Helle lost her grip on the ram's silky fleece and plunged into the crashing waves below.

A grief-stricken Phrixus continued on to Colchis, where, in gratitude, and in memory of his sister, he sacrificed the ram to Zeus, who returned it to its place among the stars. Phrixus presented its glimmering fleece to a delighted King Aeëtes, who, in turn, gave Phrixus the hand of his daughter in marriage.

★ ★ ★

So, the Golden Fleece became Aeëtes's most treasured possession. He hung it, with great ceremony, on the branch of an ancient oak tree, standing proud in a sacred grove. There it remained for untold years, while its fame spread far and wide.

When news of this gold-spun treasure reached Greece, King Pelias of Iolcos began dreaming of owning it for himself. But Pelias was not a rightful king. He had stolen the throne, ruthlessly, from his brother, Aeson, banishing Aeson and his son, Jason. Ever since, his evil deeds had haunted his waking hours, and one day, in turmoil, he decided to consult the Oracle.

"Beware a man with only one sandal," the Oracle warned him, ominously.

For years, Pelias thought nothing more of the warning, until the time came to hold games in honor of the sea god, Poseidon. Athletes and spectators from far and wide arrived in the hundreds, and among them was Jason, returned to claim what was rightfully his. At once, Pelias recognized his nephew, for Jason was wearing just one sandal—he had lost the other while helping an old woman cross the river. Remembering the Oracle's warning, Pelias promised to return Jason's throne—on one condition. Jason must sail to Colchis and bring back the fabled Golden Fleece.

In the months that followed, under the guidance of Athena, goddess of wisdom and war, Jason set to work having a great ship built. It was the finest ship ever seen. Named the Argo, it had gleaming timbers—a gift from the gods—billowing sails, and banks of oars stacked proudly on either side. Once the ship was finished, Jason picked his crew from Greece's greatest heroes, among them Heracles, Bellerophon, and Orpheus. The mighty Argonauts.

At last, Jason and his Argonauts set sail for Colchis, as difficult and dangerous a voyage as any could be. Many obstacles lay in their path, but eventually they reached the court of King Phineus and asked the wise old king his advice on what lay ahead. Solemnly, Phineus agreed to show them the way to Colchis.

"First," he said, "I need your help. My kingdom is being terrorized by harpies—monstrous birds with women's heads. They take food from my people and peck at their eyes. They will bring famine and death, and will destroy this city."

No sooner had he finished his tale than a band of harpies, clawing and shrieking with rage, swooped down and attacked the Argonauts. Yet they were no match for the Argo's time-honored heroes and were chased away, far out to sea.

A grateful King Phineus kept his side of the bargain. "To reach Colchis," he told Jason, "you must first pass through the Clashing Rocks, colossal gray cliffs that crash together, crushing any ship that tries to sail through." To avoid this fate, Phineus continued, "You must release a single dove to fly between the cliffs and trick them into slamming shut. When the cliffs reopen, your Argonauts must row with all their might and haste, before the cliffs close."

As the Argo approached the Clashing Rocks, Jason did exactly as the king advised and released a dove ahead of the ship. Aside from a few lost tail feathers, the bird made it safely through, followed by the Argonauts, heaving and straining at their oars.

Weeks turned into months, and finally, the Argo sailed into Colchis, where Jason made his way to King Aeëtes. Though the king listened patiently to Jason's story, he had no intention of giving up his precious fleece. If Jason wanted it, he told him, he must perform three tasks to prove his worth. It seemed as though

The Golden Fleece

Jason's dreams of reclaiming his throne were over, but once again the gods
came to his aid. They made the king's daughter, Medea, a sorceress, fall in love
with Jason and use her powers to help him.

Jason's first task was to plough a field with a pair of fire-breathing bulls.
Snorting flames and bellowing smoke, the oxen reared wildly, almost crushing
Jason beneath their thundering feet. Using all of his strength, Jason eventually
tamed the terrible beasts, protected from their searing breath by Medea's
magical potion.

Next, Jason had to sow the teeth of a dragon in
the newly ploughed earth. As the sun
shone down, the seeds immediately
began to break through the soil

and sprouted into a battle-crazed army of warriors. Heavily outnumbered, it seemed that Jason had met his match. Still, our hero was not ready to give up. Glancing around, he spied a rock lying near his feet. He knew what he must do. He picked up the stone and threw it into the center of the army. Not realizing where the rock had come from, the soldiers looked suspiciously at one another then began fighting among themselves, while Jason swiftly made his escape.

Although Jason had more than proved his courage, a third and deadlier task now awaited him—to steal the Golden Fleece from the sacred oak grove. This would be no easy feat as the fleece was guarded—day and night—by a dragon that never slept. Coiled serpent-like around the trunk of the tree, the creature lay, always watchful and never tired. It seemed impossible for Jason to catch it off guard. Summoning her sorcery, Medea told Jason to ask the master musician, Orpheus, to play a soothing lullaby on his lyre. Sure enough, charmed by the exquisite sound of the music, the beast closed its eyes and slumbered.

At last, Jason was able to seize the fleece and sail on the Argo for home, where he reclaimed his throne and ruled with Medea as his wife. The Argonauts, who had accompanied him so heroically, continued their daring deeds. And the Argo, Jason's trusty ship, took its place among the stars where she sails through the skies to this day.

CANIS MAJOR AND CANIS MINOR

The Dog and the Fox

A TALE FROM ANCIENT GREECE

As darkness falls, two heavenly hounds—one large, one small—can be seen racing across the night sky. The bigger star dog is the legendary Laelaps, who always catches its prey. The smaller creature is a fox so fast that it is destined never to be caught.

Named after the powerful storm-wind, Laelaps was so sweetly swift that it could outrun anything it chased. Hunters, both humans and gods, longed to own this fleet-footed beast, yet the dog belonged to Zeus, the all-seeing king of the gods. Later, Zeus gave the dog as a gift to Europa, queen of Crete, who in turn gave it to her son, Minos. But Minos and his wife had a quarrel, and she put a terrible curse on the king. He was saved by a princess called Procris and gave her the dog as a reward. He also gave her a golden spear that never missed its mark. Hunting was a favorite pastime of Procris and she could not have been more pleased by the generous gifts.

Years later, Procris married a man called Cephalus, a handsome hero and the son of a god. As a wedding gift, Procris gave her husband her most treasured possessions—the magical spear and the hunting dog, and together they set off into the forest to hunt. With a dog that always captured its prey and a spear that always hit its target, they caught deer, hare, and wild boar—too many to count. Then, tragedy struck. Distracted by a sudden noise and sensing danger, Cephalus let loose Minos's shining spear. As he watched in silent horror, the spear hit his beloved Procris, who fell down, instantly dead.

Wracked with grief and guilt at his part in his wife's death, Cephalus roamed the land and eventually arrived in Thebes. There, he heard tales of a monstrous fox that was ravaging the countryside, attacking farmers and devouring their flocks. No one had been able to catch it or kill it, though many had tried. Hoping to make amends for his crime, Cephalus vowed to help the townspeople. With a band of local hunters, he ringed the fields with a maze of nets, hoping to tangle the beast within it. But the cunning creature simply leapt over the traps, clearing the tops with a single bound. The hunters slipped their dogs off their

The Dog and the Fox

leashes and let them loose. This fox, however, was destined never to be caught, and the dogs, slathering and spent, soon gave up.

Meanwhile, Laelaps had been straining at its leash with all of its strength, and now, Cephalus let it free. With the wind at its feet, the dog gave chase, running more swiftly than an arrow's flight. Climbing to a nearby hilltop, Cephalus watched the race unfold. In no time at all, he was certain, Laelaps would bring the fox down and return. Yet, each time Laelaps caught up with the fox, the fox escaped. Stride for stride, the dog pressed ever closer, until it seemed, finally, that the fox was caught.

But, as before, just as Laelaps snapped its jaws, the fox escaped, leaving the dog biting pitifully at thin air. Minutes turned into hours, and hours into days, and still there was no end in sight for the dog that always caught what it chased and the fox that could never be caught. And so, to end the never-ending pursuit on Earth, Zeus turned both dog and fox into stone then set them in the sky as the big dog and the little dog in the stars.

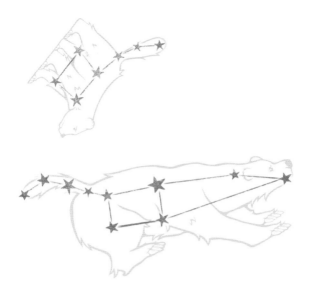

Callisto and Arcas

A TALE FROM ANCIENT GREECE

Taking pride of place in the northern night sky is Ursa Major—the Great Bear. One of the largest of all constellations, this mother keeps a close eye on her bear cub, Ursa Minor. Against the odds, they have been reunited, and she will not lose sight of him again.

Once, there was a beautiful spirit of the woods called Callisto, who served the great Artemis, goddess of hunting. Dressed in white, just like the goddess, she faithfully followed Artemis through the forest, bow in hand, roaming far and wide in search of wild animals. One day, mighty Zeus caught sight of Callisto resting in a shady grove, and, struck by her strength and grace, the king of the gods fell in love with her. By and by, Callisto gave birth to a son, called Arcas. But by falling in love she had broken the rules of Artemis's band and was forced to fend for herself in the woods.

When Zeus's wife, Hera, learned of the affair, her fury and jealousy knew

24

no bounds. Bent on revenge, she vowed to make Callisto so hideous that Zeus would not love her any more. Tracking her down to the forest, Hera grabbed Callisto and threw her to the ground. As Callisto stretched out her arms for mercy, thick dark hairs began to sprout from her skin. Her delicate hands and feet turned into huge curving claws, and her beautiful face became wide gaping jaws. When she opened her mouth to call for help, her voice had become a deep, grumbling growl.

For fifteen long years, Callisto roamed the forest as the bear she had become. Once a hunter herself, she was now hunted and hid in fear. One morning, Callisto heard the familiar sound of hunters approaching. They were tying nets to the branches to close off the gaps between the trees. Caught in their trap, she turned to see a young man aiming an arrow straight at her. Immediately, she recognized him as her son, Arcas, and ran to him, calling out his name. Unluckily for poor Callisto, all Arcas saw and heard was a huge bear, lumbering towards him, as if to attack. In fear, not knowing that it was his mother, the boy bent back his bow, ready to shoot the glassy-eyed beast . . .

Just in time, fate, and the gods, intervened. As Arcas prepared to release his arrow, Zeus transformed him into a bear cub so that he could understand his mother's cries. Then, the king of the gods grabbed them both by their tails and swung them up to the heavens so they could live in peace among the stars—the big bear and the little bear.

HERACLES

The Labors of Heracles

A TALE FROM ANCIENT GREECE

Kneeling among the stars, mighty club in mighty hand, shines Heracles, the greatest of all Greek heroes. Famed for his superhuman size and strength, he has been cast into the sky by his father, Zeus, for triumphing against impossible odds.

Half man, half god, Heracles was the son of Zeus and Alcmene, a wise and beautiful mortal woman. Their love affair left Zeus's wife, Hera, bitterly jealous, and she resented Heracles from the moment he was born. As the years passed, Zeus grew ever prouder of his son's strength and courage, while Hera, poisoned with envy, vowed to make Heracles's life miserable. Several times Hera tried to kill him, once sending a pair of colossal snakes to attack him in his crib. Calmly, Heracles seized each snake in turn and strangled it with his bare hands.

As a young man, Heracles married Megara, daughter of the King of Thebes, and had two children whom he dearly loved. Now, Hera saw her chance for revenge. Summoning spells and sorcery, she drove poor Heracles insane, and in his madness, he killed his wife and children. When the madness passed, Heracles was horrified by the dreadful deed he had done. Filled with grief and despair, he fled to Delphi to consult the Oracle about how he could make amends.

"You must seek out Eurystheus, king of Mycenae," the Oracle ordered. "Serve the king for ten years, and do anything and everything he asks."

So, Heracles made his way to Mycenae, his fate in the king's hands. Unluckily for our hero, the king was guided by Hera, and, as punishment, he set Heracles ten labors that, at first glance, seemed impossible. If Heracles completed all ten tasks, he would be freed from his guilt. If he failed, he was doomed for all eternity to suffer in torment, knowing neither peace nor rest. So began an extraordinary journey that took Heracles to every part of the known world.

First, the king sent him to Nemea to slay a monstrous lion, the terror of the land. Twice as big as a normal lion, its skin was so tough that no weapon had ever pierced it. In vain, Heracles fought the beast with his faithful club, but his brave efforts left no mark. Thinking quickly, he backed the lion into its lair where he strangled it to death using his bare hands, then used the beast's own claws to cut off its hide. Later, Zeus set the lion into the sky as the constellation of Leo.

Wearing the lion's impenetrable skin as a cloak, Heracles journeyed to the swamps of Lerna, where a hideous nine-headed serpent, the Hydra, preyed on passersby. Heracles set to work, yet no sooner had he cut off one of the Hydra's heads than another two grew in its place. With the help of his nephew, Iolaus, Heracles sealed each bloody stump with a burning branch and so, finally, stopped the heads from growing back. With a single blow of his sword, he lopped off the last head—which was immortal—and buried it, still thrashing and writhing, under a huge rock. This same head later took its place among the stars, destined to live forever as the celestial Hydra.

The Labors of Heracles

Next, Eurystheus ordered Heracles to capture two animals that had never been caught before—an enormous deer with golden antlers and a wild boar with terrifying tusks. It was said that the deer could run fast enough to outpace an arrow and, for a whole year, Heracles chased it across Greece, until, utterly exhausted, it ran into his net. The boar—which was bigger than any other boar in the whole of Greece—he chased to the very top of Mount Erymanthus then drove it into a deep snowdrift from which it could not escape.

For his fifth task, Heracles traveled to Elis and the stables of King Augeas. Home to hundreds of the kingdom's finest cattle, the stables had not been cleaned for years. Everywhere lay deep in stinking, steaming piles of dung. Heracles struck a bargain with the king—he would clean the stables in a single day in return for some of the king's cattle. It was impossible. Not even heroic Heracles could do this alone. Working quickly, he dug a channel across the yard to two rivers that flowed nearby. Augeas looked on in disbelief as the river water rushed down the channel and through the stables, washing the filth away.

For his sixth trial, Heracles was sent to the foul-smelling Lake Stymphalia, home to a flock of man-eating birds with ripping claws, bronze beaks, and sharp metallic feathers that they fired at their victims like darts. They terrorized the land, devouring humans, destroying crops, and poisoning the earth with their dung. Undeterred, Heracles approached the ferocious flock, but the ground was too marshy to support his weight. Once more, goddess Athena stepped in, handing Heracles a pair of brass rattles. As he shook the rattles, they made such a terrible noise that the birds took flight. Taking aim, Heracles shot each and every last one of them with arrows tipped with poison from the blood of the monster Hydra.

The four tasks that followed again tested Heracles's hunting and fighting skills. In Crete, he captured a fearsome, fire-breathing bull that was rampaging

29

across the land. From there, he journeyed to Thrace to round up a herd of horses that ran wild and ate human flesh. The next labor took Heracles to the land of the Amazons—a race of mighty warrior women—to steal a magical belt belonging to their queen. Finally, he sailed to the end of the world to steal a herd of cattle from the three-headed giant Geryon, grandson of Medusa. Heracles killed Geryon with an arrow that pierced all three of his heads with one shot, then drove the cattle back to Greece.

With all ten labors completed, against all of the odds and more, Heracles eagerly returned to King Eurystheus to claim his pardon. But the cowardly king refused to keep the promise he had made. "You have cheated," he blustered. "Iolaus helped you to kill the Hydra, and, what's more, you took payment for cleaning the stables."

As punishment, the king set Heracles two further tasks, even more deadly and difficult than before. The first was to steal the golden fruit that grew on a branching apple tree in Hera's mountainside garden. The tree was guarded by a hundred-headed dragon that twisted and coiled around its trunk. The only person able to get close to the creature was the giant, Atlas, condemned to carry the weight of the world on his shoulders for eternity. Seeing Atlas, Heracles seized his chance. He offered to take the world for a while, if Atlas fetched the apples for him. However, when Atlas returned with the golden fruit, he refused to take his heavy burden back. Heracles thought quickly. "Of course, you must be weary," he said. "Let me first adjust my cloak. It will only take a moment." As Atlas rested the world back upon his shoulders, trickster Heracles swiftly made his escape.

For his twelfth, and final, labor, the king sent Heracles deep, deep into the Underworld to capture Cerberus, a vicious three-headed dog. This hellish hound guarded the gates to the land of the dead, stopping lost souls from departing.

Hades, god of the dead, gave Heracles permission to take the dog on the condition that he did not use any weapons. Protected by his lion-skin cloak, Heracles wrestled the beast to the ground and dragged it, thrashing and slathering, all the way to the court of Eurystheus.

The king was furious—he had never expected to see Heracles alive again. This time, he could not go back on his promise. Reluctantly, he released Heracles from his terrible guilt and made him a free man once more. Later, the gods granted our hero immortality, and he took his place on Mount Olympus with his father, Zeus, before rising to the northern skies to shine among the greatest stars.

ANDROMEDA

Andromeda and the Sea Monster

A TALE FROM ANCIENT GREECE

Stretched out across the evening sky, one group of stars forms the shape of a beautiful girl, bound by chains. This is Andromeda, a royal princess, being sacrificed to the sea monster Cetus, who lurks menacingly nearby. Close, too, is Perseus, her heroic husband-to-be, who will save her life.

The daughter of King Cepheus and Queen Cassiopeia of Ethiopia, Andromeda was famed for her beauty. Yet, while the king doted quietly on his daughter, the queen was vain and fond of boasting. One day, she claimed to all who cared to hear that her daughter was lovelier even than the Nereids—the exquisite sea spirits in red-coral crowns and sand-white robes who accompanied Poseidon, god of the sea.

When Poseidon heard the queen's ill-guarded words, he was filled with rage.

Andromeda and the Sea Monster

To teach her a lesson, he called on Cetus, a terrible sea creature with monstrous jaws and a coiling body covered in silver scales. Cetus was commanded to ravage the coast of Ethiopia, whipping up waves and raising floods that devastated the land. In despair, the terrified people called on their king for help. And so, Cepheus consulted the Oracle and begged the gods, with all his heart, to guide him.

"Sacrifice your daughter to Cetus," the Oracle said. "There is no other way to save your kingdom."

The heartbroken king had no choice—he must do as the Oracle ordered. While his wife looked on, now in bitter remorse, he ordered Andromeda to be chained to a rock in the sea. There he left her, softly weeping, as she prepared to die.

At that very moment, flying through the air on winged sandals, a gift from the gods, came the great hero Perseus. Fresh from slaying Medusa, he was returning home when he sighted Andromeda, standing as still as a marble statue, her soft hair stirring on the breeze. Captivated by her beauty, and anguished by her plight, Perseus asked her name. At first, Andromeda was too afraid to speak—instead, her eyes overflowed with tears—but, eventually, she

Andromeda and the Sea Monster

told Perseus her sorry story. Before she could finish speaking, a brooding gray head and shining neck rose from the sea, parting the waves as it surged towards her like a colossal ship.

As Andromeda's screams rang out, Perseus seized his sword and called to her parents, who clung pitifully to the rock.

"Let me marry your daughter," he said, "and I will rescue her from this beast."

By now the sea monster was so close, Andromeda could feel its foul, festering breath. Without delay, Perseus swooped down and drove his sword into the creature's barnacle-encrusted flesh. Letting out a deafening roar, wounded Cetus reared up then twisted around, snapping wildly at his attacker. Again and again, the hero struck, flying swiftly out of the way of its menacing jaws. With the creature bloodied and tiring, Perseus struck his final, mortal blow. At last, Cetus collapsed and sank to the depths of the ocean, never to be seen again.

Soon afterwards, to much rejoicing, Andromeda and Perseus were married. A great feast was held, with music and dancing. As Perseus entertained the guests with tales of his gorgon-slaying exploits, a commotion broke out in the hall. The king's brother, Phineus, bragging and blustering, claimed that he, not Perseus, was meant to marry Andromeda. Quick as a flash, Perseus took out Medusa's head and turned Phineus to stone.

In time, Andromeda bade farewell to her parents and followed Perseus to Greece. They had many children and lived happily, and ruled long and well. And when Andromeda and Perseus died, the gods placed them in the skies as stars, shining brightly alongside Cassiopeia, out of reach of Cetus's deadly coils.

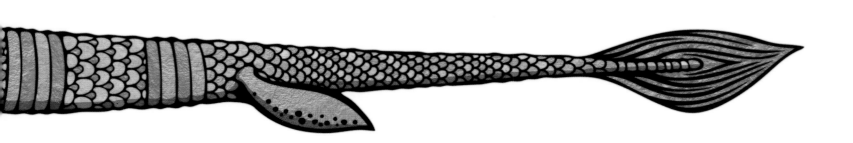

NANURJUK AND QIMMIIT (TAURUS)

The Polar Bear and the Three Runners

AN INUIT TALE

Since time began, Inuit hunters have lived in awe of mighty Nanuk, the ghost-white polar bear. It is Nanuk who decides if a hunt will be fruitful, and for this, the Inuit show their respect by offering their weapons to the bear's soul. Seen by day crossing the ice on fur-soled paws, at night, Nanuk shines brightly among the stars, outrunning its pursuers across the skies.

Once, in the far-flung North, a woman left behind her husband and home, and headed off across the ice to live among the polar bears. The bears treated her kindly and brought her meat to eat from the seals that they hunted. But as the seasons changed and the year passed, the woman grew lonely. She missed her family and her old life, and longed to return to visit them. Reluctantly, the bears agreed—on one condition. She must not tell anyone that she lived

38

among them, or let their secret location be known. Solemnly, the woman made her promise and gladly set off for home.

For a while, all was well. Until, one day, the bears spied the dread sight of hunters in the distance, racing across the snow in their dog-drawn sleds. The woman had broken her promise and brought death and danger into their midst. As the bears fled the hunters' spears, five slavering, spittle-flecked dogs were let loose to give chase. Breaking away, Nanuk, the master of the bears, ran faster and faster across the ice, the dogs in deadly pursuit, until they reached the very edge of the world and plunged into the sky. There, they appear to this day—the brightly shining star that is the bear (Nanurjuk), surrounded by a glittering circle of chase-hungry dogs (Qimmiit).

Many suns and moons later, four hunters spotted the bear glinting in the night sky. Brave-hearted, the hunters climbed up and up, until the bear was almost within reach. Quickening their pace, they began to give chase, speeding, spears ready, across the black. As they ran, one hunter dropped his mittens, which fell through the deep and dark to the ground, far, far below.

Realizing that his mittens were gone, the hunter clambered back, down and down, to Earth, leaving his three friends to continue their quest. In doing so, he became the only one of the hunters to make it back to their camp, while the others remain forever in the sky as three stars. To the Inuit they are known as Ullaktut; to others they are the three stars in the belt of Orion. Look closely and below them you can see their star children, carrying warm clothes of caribou skin for their fathers and growing cold from running across the dark night.

THE SUN

Grandmother Spider and the Sun

A CHEROKEE TALE

Many tales are told about the Sun and its daily journey across the sky. The Cherokee people look back to the dark time before the Sun shone and how a group of animals brought sunlight to the world.

In the beginning, when the world was new, there was only darkness all around. Life was difficult for people and animals. It was cold and they were miserable, forever bumping into each other because they could not see. Something had to be done, and, in the deep forest, the animals gathered together.

"I've heard tell of something called the Sun," a low voice growled out of the dark. It was Bear. "It gives out light and is warm, too. It is kept on the other side of the Earth, but the people who guard it are too greedy to share. Perhaps we could steal a piece of it?"

Grandmother Spider and the Sun

All of the animals nodded their heads and agreed that this was a fine idea. But who would be the one to steal the Sun? Who would do this daring deed? One by one, a few brave animals stepped forward, while the others hid in the woods to watch. The first to try was Fox. Stealthily, on soft-furred paws, he crept to the secret place where the Sun was kept. Silent and still, he waited until no one was watching then grabbed the Sun in his mouth and started to run for his life. But the Sun was so scorchingly hot it scalded Fox's mouth and he dropped it. That is why, to this day, all foxes have black mouths.

The next animal to try was Opossum. Now, in those long-ago days, opossums had long, bushy tails. And so, proud Opossum sneaked up to the place where unfortunate Fox had dropped the Sun and ran back with it balanced on her magnificent tail. But the Sun was so searingly hot it scorched away all of the hair on her tail, and, just like Fox, she dropped it. That is why, to this day, all opossums have long, bare tails.

Just when the quest seemed hopeless, Grandmother Spider scurried out of the bushes. Although she was much smaller than the other animals, she was clever. "Might I try?" she asked, quietly. And, instead of trying to hold on to the fiery ball, she wove a fine silk bag from one of her dew-draped webs. When she found the Sun, she dropped it carefully into her bag and carried it back without burning herself. Everyone began to rejoice, yet one important question remained—where was the Sun to go?

Grandmother Spider had the answer: "We should put the Sun high in the sky," she said. "That way, everyone will see it and benefit from its light."

It was perfect, agreed all the animals. However, try as hard as they could to reach and leap, none of them were tall enough to reach the sky. Then, Buzzard swooped down on his great feathered wings.

Grandmother Spider and the Sun

"I can fly higher than any bird," he said. "I will carry the Sun into the sky."

The Sun was still blazing, even inside its silk bag, so Buzzard placed it on top of his head, where his feathers were thickest. He began to fly, higher and higher, above the clouds. Yet the higher he flew, the hotter the Sun grew, and it began to burn through the silk. Even so, Buzzard kept flying, up and up, until all the feathers on his head were gone. Still he kept flying, even as the skin on his head began to turn red, until, finally, he reached the very top of the sky and placed the Sun there, for all to see. This is why, to this day, some buzzards have bald, red heads.

As the Sun's rays streaked across the sky, like the strands of Grandmother Spider's woven web, the world below was bathed in sunlight and warmth, and animals and people rejoiced. And Buzzard was honored for bringing light to the sky and can still be seen circling around the Sun today.

How Fisher Brought Summer

AN ANISHINAABE TALE

Seven bright stars in Ursa Major make the shape of a plough, a saucepan, or a bear pursued by hunters, depending on how you look. Some tribes in North America see a creature called a fisher, with an arrow caught in its tail.

Many suns and moons ago, it was always winter on Earth. There was no spring and no summer, and never any sun or warmth. Snow covered the land and icy cold seeped into freezing bones.

In the snow-laden woods lived Fisher, a fox-like creature with a sleek slender body and soft fur tail. Small and fierce, he was an expert hunter, and each day he went in search of squirrels to feed his family, for they were weary with hunger. But the winds were too harsh and the snow too deep, and for a long time he had no luck at all. At last, Fisher spied a squirrel, thin and shivering

45

with cold, just like him. Before he could pounce, the squirrel spoke to him:

"Don't kill me great hunter," she said. "I have some advice for you. If you do as I tell you and spare me, you can bring summer back to the world. There will be food for all of us, and you will be your people's pride."

Hunger gnawed at Fisher, but he listened carefully to the squirrel's words. Then, he made his way home and invited all of his friends to hear what he planned to do.

"I shall make the journey to the place we call Skyland," he told them. "Where it is closest to the Earth. There, people have all the warmth and food they could ever possibly need. I shall bring summer back with me and end this long, bitter winter, before we all starve."

When Fisher had finished speaking, his friends cheered and some of them offered to travel with him on his adventure. Fisher chose the strongest among them—Otter, Lynx, and Wolverine—and the four of them set off into the white wilderness. For many long days, they traveled towards the mountains, climbing higher and higher each day, and sleeping each night under a blanket of snow. It grew bitterly cold and the wind scraped their faces, until finally, they reached the highest peak, where the sky was so close they could almost touch it. Now, they had to find a way to break through and reach the sun-soaked land above.

"We'll take turns to jump," said Fisher. "Who wants to go first?"

Otter was the first to try. She leaped up and touched the sky but couldn't break through. She fell back to Earth and slid on her soft smooth belly all the way to the bottom of the mountain. Next, Lynx tried; followed by Fisher. Neither had the strength to make even the tiniest chink.

"It's your turn," Fisher said to Wolverine. "You're the strongest of us all."

Wolverine leapt as high as he could and struck the sky, hard. Again and

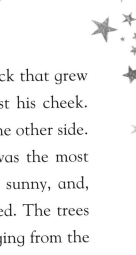

again, he jumped up and hit the sky, until finally, he made a crack that grew bigger and bigger. He smiled as he felt a warm breeze rush past his cheek. The hole was big enough now for him to crawl right through to the other side. One by one, the animals followed Wolverine into Skyland. It was the most beautiful place they had ever seen. The weather was gloriously sunny, and, all around, sweet-smelling flowers and plants of all kinds bloomed. The trees were not bare and leafless, but laden with berries and fruit. Hanging from the branches were cages with birds of every color that filled the air with the sound of birdsong. Fisher released the birds and they flew down to Earth through the crack in the sky. Then the friends set to work making the hole even bigger so that the warmth of Skyland could flood through to the world below, melting the snow drip by drip and allowing fresh green grass to peek through.

When the Sky People saw what they were doing, they ran after them, furious, to try to stop them from stealing their precious summer days. Wolverine escaped back through the hole in the sky, shouting to Fisher to follow him. But Fisher did not listen. Instead, as the Sky People came closer, he busied himself making the hole bigger and bigger, so that they could not close it and plunge the Earth into winter once more. By the time the Sky People reached him, the hole in the sky was big enough for warm weather to slip through for half of the year, bringing summer, but not for summer to last all year round. Frantically, the Sky People tried to stop him, shooting showers of arrows. As a fatal arrow struck him, Fisher rolled on his back and began to fall…

But Fisher never reached the Earth far below. The gods took pity on him, and as a reward for his great sacrifice on behalf of his people, they set him high in the sky among the stars. There, he can be seen throughout the year, rolling on to his back in winter and jumping to his feet as springtime comes.

THE MILKY WAY

How Coyote Scattered the Stars

A NAVAJO TALE

In the parched desert landscape of the American Southwest, the night sky reaches out to touch the Earth in all directions, cloaking it in countless stars. Under these skies, Navajo people built their hogans, or homes, spread their blankets on the ground, and told stories about the stars.

Long, long ago, when the Earth was young, the Navajo gods met in the hogan of creation. They painted the Sun and Moon on the new sky and divided day from night. But they noticed that the night sky still looked dark and bare, even with the luminous light of the Moon. As they debated what to do, Black God, god of fire, arrived in the doorway, dressed all in black, with a buckskin mask charred by sacred flames, a crescent moon on his forehead, and a full moon for his mouth. Attached to his ankle was a small cluster of twinkling stars, the likes of which the gods had never seen before. Curious, they asked Black God what they were.

Without saying a word, Black God walked slowly around the hogan. As he reached the north side he stopped and stamped his foot hard on the ground so that the stars on his ankle sprang, sparkling, to his knee. Then he went, in turn, to the east, south, and west, stamping his foot each time. From his knee, each star leapt on to his hip, up to his shoulder, and finally on to his temple. And there they remain, to this day, painted in pride of place on Black God's buckskin mask.

The other gods were filled with amazement.

"What are these strange crystals?" they asked, in delight. "They are beautiful."

Black God answered, "They are called stars."

The gods debated among themselves then quickly agreed. They asked Black God to make more stars to sprinkle in the deep, dark night sky to make it more beautiful. So, Black God pulled out a pouch that he carried always, made from the finest fawn-skin and filled with countless crystals. From the pouch, he took out a single crystal that shone bright and clear. He reached up and placed it, ever so carefully, in the north sky. This became North Fire, the star that guides travelers and keeps them safe.

Near North Fire, Black God placed the crystal figures of a man and woman. These were Revolving Male and Revolving Female, set to circle forever around North Fire. Their spinning path would mark out the shape of a hogan, with North Fire as the heart of the home. Next, Black God turned to the east, south, and west, decorating the sky with more patterns—Man with Feet Spread Apart, Rabbit Tracks, and Horned Rattler—each one placed precisely and perfectly.

After this, he fashioned a copy of the pattern of stars at his temple and placed them, too, in the sky. Reaching once more into his pouch, he pulled out thousands of tiny crystals and, with a flourish, scattered them across the darkness.

After Black God had finished filling the sky with star patterns, he placed some of his own fire in the heavens to light up the stars. The other gods gasped in admiration—the sky was beautiful indeed. Just as Black God sat down to admire his work, the trickster Coyote appeared, bent on making mischief.

"What have you been doing here?" Coyote cried. "No one asked my opinion! You should have waited for me."

"See for yourself," Black God replied. "We have created patterns in the skies and rules for people to follow. We didn't need your help."

Then Black God finally sat down and was about to place his precious pouch under his foot, for protection.

"We'll see about that," said cunning Coyote, grinning wildly, as he reached over and snatched the bag away. Coyote opened the pouch and blew the rest of the crystals far and wide across the sky. They fell as thousands of scattered stars, shimmering and tumbling in a jumble of light and disorder. Laughing, Coyote looked into the pouch and found one last crystal.

"This will be my own star," he said, and, mimicking Black God, he reached high in the sky and carefully placed the star in the south. "Now the skies are truly beautiful."

And this is how the stars came to be as they are today. The patterns so thoughtfully placed by Black God bring order and guidance to people on Earth. But the rest of the sky is filled with chaos and disorder, apart from the Coyote Star. For the Navajo, these two aspects of the night sky reflect the balance between order and chaos of life itself.

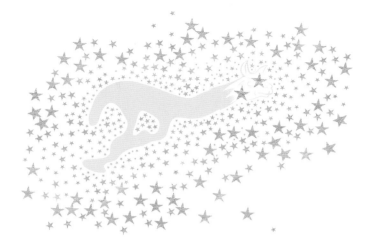

The Llama Star

AN INCAN TALE

To the Incas of South America, the dark patches that mottle the Milky Way were living creatures come to drink from the river of stars. Among them, between the Southern Cross and Scorpio, were two llamas—a starry-eyed mother and her suckling baby. Llamas were of great importance to the Incas, and herders offered sacrifices, both to the earthly animals and their heavenly counterparts.

An ancient Inca tale tells how, long ago, people on Earth became cruel and greedy. They were so busy fighting and stealing from one another that they forgot to tend their fields and crops, or to worship their gods. The only place where humans still led good, god-filled lives was high up in the Andes, on the rocky mountain slopes. Here lived two brothers—honest, hard-working llama herders of the highest character. The brothers knew their llamas, every one, as well as themselves, and now they were worried. For days, the llamas had been acting strangely, refusing to eat their food and spending long, mournful nights gazing up at the stars. Deeply puzzled, the brothers asked the llamas to tell them what was wrong.

"The stars have warned us," replied the llamas, "that the gods are angry. To punish people for their wickedness, they are planning to send a furious flood that will destroy every creature that lives on Earth."

At once, the brothers moved their flocks and families to safety in caves higher up the mountain, where the rest of the animal world had gathered. No sooner had they taken shelter, then the rain began to fall like nothing ever seen before. Clouds turned the day as black as night. Thunder rumbled; licks of lightning streaked across the sky. Still the rain came. The brothers saw that the llamas had been right. Looking down from the lofty peaks, they watched as rivers burst their banks and washed the world and its pitiful people away.

As the waters rose, miraculously, the llama herders' mountain grew taller and taller. Even so, water soon began to lap at their cave door, and worse, their provisions were running low. Then, one day, as the brothers peeked out, they saw that the rain had stopped and the glowering screen of clouds had cleared. Once again, Inti, the sun god, appeared in the sky and smiled, causing the waters to dry up and disappear. The herders' mountain shrunk down to its normal height, and the herders and their families returned to Earth, which they soon filled with their children and their grandchildren.

Meanwhile, in the stars, the mother llama and her baby look down on the world and its people and are worshipped as gods in return. At night, when the world below is sleeping, the llama climbs down from the sky and drinks the water out of the ocean to stop the seas from overflowing. And, while people live almost everywhere on Earth, llamas still remember the days and nights of the flood and always prefer to live on higher ground.

The Sun God and the Snake

A TALE FROM ANCIENT EGYPT

In Ancient Egypt, Ra, mighty Sun god, was the most powerful of all deities. In his honor, the Egyptians told stories about how he created the world and sailed across the sky each day, causing the Sun to rise and set.

In the beginning, there was no land in Egypt, only inky blackness and a vast watery waste. Then, slowly, out of the darkness, a huge shining egg arose, and out of the egg came Ra, the greatest of all the gods. As Ra appeared, the Sun rose into the sky for the first time. Then, Ra set the first winds to blow and the first rain to fall. He made the Earth and placed above it the gentle arch of the sky. Next, Ra set the River Nile to flow through Egypt, bringing fertility to the land. After that, he filled the Earth with plants and animals, and finally, with people themselves.

The Sun God and the Snake

His work of creation completed, Ra took the shape of a man and became the first pharaoh of Egypt. For countless thousands of years, he ruled wisely and well, bringing such plentiful harvests that people spoke of them forever afterwards. In time, however, Ra grew old, and people no longer obeyed his laws. Instead, they mocked him, cruelly, for the way his gray head shook with age and his wizened mouth dribbled as he ate.

The gods knew that they could not seize Ra's throne unless they knew his secret name, for it held the key to his powers, past, present, and future. So the goddess Isis hatched a cunning plan. She collected some of Ra's saliva that had fallen from his mouth onto the earth, and she mixed it with water to make clay. Then, she formed the clay into the shape of a snake—the very first cobra—which became, from that moment on, the symbol of royalty. Unseen and unnoticed, Isis placed the cobra by the side of the dust-dry road that Ra traveled each day to inspect his kingdom. One day, as Ra passed by, the cobra—hood spread—reared up and bit him on the leg.

The snake's deadly poison coursed through Ra's body, making him cry out in dreadful agony. One minute he burned with fiery fever; the next, icy chills made him shiver and tremble. Ra was puzzled by what had happened. Had he not created everything that lived on Earth? How, then, had he been hurt by a creature that he had not made? In his distress, he called on the gods of healing to come swiftly to his aid, and come they did. First to arrive was Isis, who smiled to see her scheming so well rewarded.

"Great Father," she said, slyly, "I will use my magic to help you. First, you must tell me your secret Name of Power. For it is only by using this name in my spells that I can cure your pain."

In reply, suffering Ra spoke many names to her.

The Sun God and the Snake

"I am Creator of the Earth and Sky. I am Maker of Mountains. I am Source of all Rivers and Lakes. I am Light and Darkness. I am the Sun that burns in the sky..."

Still, Isis spoke not a word and uttered no spell, and the poison continued to flow. For Ra had told her the names that all people knew and not the secret name, hidden in his heart. More powerfully the poison burned, more terrible than any flame or fire, until Ra could stand it no longer and cried out:

"So be it! I will tell you. May the Name of Power pass into your heart!"

"By the Name of Power," Isis replied at once, "let the poison be gone."

At last, Ra was cured of his snakebite and found peace from the pain, though his rule on Earth was now ended. Instead, he took his place high up in the heavens as the Sun, and there he remains. By day, he sails serenely across the sky in his golden boat, flanked by companions, giving light to the world from dawn to dusk. By night, he leaves the sky and the world in darkness, as he sails down through the Underworld, his boat now carrying the prayers of the living, along with the souls of the dead. Here, he must conquer the demon-serpent, Apep, his sworn and greatest enemy, who lies in wait with his servant, a monstrous crocodile, to block the gods' path.

Each night, as battle begins, blind Apep, with his unseeing stare, sways to and fro, to and fro, as he tries to hypnotize the gods, before devouring them. But the gods are always ready. For if Apep is allowed victory the world will descend into dark chaos. They trap the beast with ropes and nets, chanting spells and incantations to keep him subdued so that they can slay him. And so, every night, victorious, Ra's boat continues on its way, carrying the Sun into the sky to light up the world for another day.

ORION

The Pharaoh's Soul

A TALE FROM ANCIENT EGYPT

Across the world, stargazers marvel at the figure of Orion striding across the heavens. In Ancient Greece he is a mythical hunter. In Ancient Egypt he is the great god Osiris, ruler of death and the afterlife.

Many suns and moons ago, mighty Geb, god of earth, and Nut, goddess of sky, had four children—Osiris, Isis, Set, and Nephthys. Osiris, the eldest, was good and wise, and, for these and other qualities, he was named Pharaoh of Egypt by the all-powerful sun god, Ra. For many years, Osiris ruled well and fairly, with beautiful Isis as his queen, setting order above chaos and justice above lawlessness. He taught people to farm successfully and to live peacefully, and his deeds earned him the love and respect of the gods and of all those who lived on Earth.

But not everyone fell under Osiris's spell. His brother, Set, god of storms and chaos, was deeply jealous of the Pharaoh's popularity and power, and hatched

a devious plot to kill him. Set knew that he had to be clever about it—Osiris was nobody's fool—so he decided to hold a feast in Osiris's honor, to thank him for all that he done for his people and his land.

"After all," scheming Set told anyone who would listen, "he never stops working and doing good; now it's his turn to reap the rewards."

The feast was one of the most lavish ever held in Egypt; only the finest food and drink were served. There was singing, dancing, and games, and, from his seat of honor, Osiris smiled broadly as he surveyed the scene. After everyone had eaten and drank their fill, Set clapped his hands loudly for order, and his servants brought out an exquisite chest made from sweet-smelling cedar wood, intricately carved and decorated with bright colors and sheets of gold, as if by the gods.

"I have one final game for you," Set announced to the guests, smiling slyly. "I will give this chest to whoever can fit inside."

One by one, the courtiers climbed into the chest, each hoping to claim it as their own. None of them fit, of course. Next, Osiris decided to try. The chest fit him perfectly—after all, it had been made, secretly, and especially, for him. As soon as Osiris was inside, Set gave a triumphant roar, slammed down the lid, and sealed it shut. Then, he had it thrown into the River Nile, where it drifted on the current all the way to the Mediterranean Sea, until it was finally cast ashore. And, while all of Egypt mourned the loss of their faithful king, Set claimed the throne for himself.

Grieving Isis wept bitter tears for her husband and the fate he had suffered at Set's hand. For a full year, she roamed the land far and wide, searching for his resting place. One day, as hope had almost faded, she came across a tamarisk tree on a distant riverbank that had grown up, gnarled and mighty, around the

chest. Taking the form of a magnificent kite, Isis, bird goddess, flew around the chest, clapping her gilded wings. Singing a kite's shrill song of mourning, she carried it back home and hid it among the thick reeds of the marshes. It was there that Set saw the chest, glinting and glittering in the sun, and wreaked his vile revenge. Furiously pulling Osiris's body from the chest, he cut it into pieces and scattered them far and wide.

"And that truly is the end of him," he sniggered.

Next morning, Isis returned to the marshes to perform rituals for the dead, only to find the body gone. Transforming once more into a golden-winged bird, she flew high over Egypt, until she had gathered up all the pieces of Osiris's body. With the help of Anubis, jackal-headed god of embalming, she began the painstaking task of putting the pieces back together. Night after night they

The Pharaoh's Soul

worked, until the body was whole again. They wrapped it in white-linen strips as a mummy, as was fitting for a pharaoh. Then Isis performed her greatest magic. Flapping her shimmering wings, she fanned breath into her husband's body and brought him back to life.

But no spirit that has once passed to the land of the dead can remain in the land of the living, and so the sun god, Ra, decreed that Osiris should be Lord of the Afterlife. With this, Osiris became the lord of the dead and the god of rebirth—proof that new life can come, even after death. And his soul passed into the heavens, where it was taken up among the stars—his starry belt aligned, some say, with the great pyramids of Giza, resting place of pharaohs.

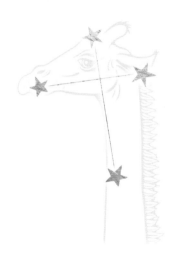

How Giraffe Became a Star

A BUSHMAN TALE, AFRICA

As night falls over Southern Africa, a sparkling blanket of stars appears in the sky. Chief among them are four bright stars that make up the constellation of Crux, also known as the Southern Cross. Visible year round in the southern hemisphere, people have, over thousands of years, given this star pattern many names. Some see in the stars the shape of a cross; some see a pouncing pride of lions. The Tswana people see the outstretched necks of giraffes, transported from the Earth below to roam the rolling grasslands of heaven.

Long ago, when the world was still young, the sky was a dome of gray-blue rock, resting on the Earth beneath it. The Sun moved, daily, across the dome, while at night the stars twinkled through holes in the rock. At that time, the animals on Earth, big and small, were each given a task to carry out, depending

on their size, shape, and talents. With their sharp teeth and claws, lions were set to guard, while elephants, for their great strength, were put in charge of moving logs. Soon, everyone had something useful to do . . . except for Giraffe. With no real skills to set him apart, Giraffe idled away most of his days, staring mournfully up into the sky. While the other animals went busily about their work, Giraffe was left behind, too tall and too clumsy to help.

The other animals looked on sadly at their friend and wracked their brains to think of something that Giraffe could do. Then, one day, they had a brilliant idea. They realized that because Giraffe was so tall and always had his head in the clouds, he could be helpful, after all. They had noticed that the Sun kept getting lost in the heavens, bumping up and down, this way and that, on its path across the sky. It needed someone to keep it on its arching track. With his long neck and legs, Giraffe was perfect—the only animal that could reach up so high. So, without delay, Giraffe was put to work. All day long, Giraffe stared at the sky, guiding the Sun and making sure that it never lost its way again. If the Sun ever veered off track, Giraffe simply stretched his long neck high above the clouds and gave it a gentle nudge.

Delighted to have a purpose at last, Giraffe took his job very seriously. In fact, he did it so often, and so well, that he was honored with the finest reward. Some of the stars were rearranged to always point in the Sun's direction. The Bushmen named the star pattern "Tutwa" (Giraffe) and they use it still to guide them as they travel through the night. They remind us all, forever, that everyone has something that sets them apart.

Gilgamesh and the Bull

A SUMERIAN TALE

In the night sky, the ancient Sumerians saw a hunter, mighty Gilgamesh. Part-god, part-human, he was the greatest king that had ever lived. Nearby loomed the shape of a gigantic bull, the Bull of Heaven, forever locked in mortal combat with the king.

When the gods created Gilgamesh—king of Uruk—they made him two-thirds man and one-third god. He was wise and he was strong, but he was also proud and arrogant. Together with his faithful friend, once enemy, Enkidu, Gilgamesh fought monsters and moved mountains, yet greater fame and fortune always beckoned. So, one day, despite the gods' warnings, Gilgamesh and Enkidu journeyed to the enchanted Cedar Forest—home of the gods—and killed its monstrous guardian, the giant Humbaba.

When Gilgamesh returned to Uruk in triumph, he washed himself in the river, dressed in fine clean robes, and placed his golden crown upon his head.

Gilgamesh and the Bull

Then, he made offerings to Shamash, god of the Sun, for his victory and safe return. Lost in thoughts of glory, he did not notice the beguiling goddess of love, Ishtar, watching.

"Gilgamesh," she said, "You are not only heroic but handsome. There is no other man like you. Marry me, I order you. If you do, I will make you a chariot with wheels of gold, pulled by the fleetest storm demons. Kings and princes will bow down before you, if you will be my husband."

Gilgamesh looked at her, in all of her enchanting beauty, and smiled.

"Goddess, although I am truly flattered," he said, "I must refuse. I shall worship you always as a goddess, but I cannot have you as my wife. Anyone you have ever loved has been cast aside once you have lost interest in them. You have turned them into creatures—wolves and moles—or left them broken beyond repair."

When Ishtar heard his words, she flew into a furious temper, storming and stamping with rage. Rushing to heaven, she flung herself, weeping, at her father's feet.

"My father," she sobbed, "Gilgamesh must be punished. He has insulted me and must pay. Give me Gugalanna, the Bull of Heaven, to destroy him once and for all."

"Dear daughter," replied her father, the sky god, Anu, "ask anything of me, but not this. If I let loose the Bull of Heaven, there will be seven years of drought in Uruk and the harvests will fail. Innocent people will go hungry; many of them will die. Have you thought of the suffering you will cause?"

"The city's stores are full," hissed Ishtar. "There is plenty of grain for the people and plenty of hay for the animals. Besides, if you don't give me what I want, I will break open the doors of Hell and release the souls of the dead on the world."

Gilgamesh and the Bull

Even mighty Anu shivered to hear her bone-chilling words, uttered with such cold menace. He knew that Ishtar would stop at nothing to get her own way. So, with heavy heart, he released the Bull of Heaven and gave it to his daughter to lead to the gates of Uruk.

In the city, deep disquiet and foreboding soon gave way to heart-stopping fear. From the gates came the shouts of guards, crying that the end of the world was here. From high on the city walls, Gilgamesh and Enkidu watched in horror as Ishtar led the bull, as big as a herd of elephants, down to the river. Its snorting set buildings shaking and crumbling to dust, and the stamping of its huge hooved feet opened up such gaping cracks in the ground that hundreds of people were swallowed up.

As the Bull passed beneath them, in a flash, Enkidu leapt down from the wall and landed between its monstrous horns. Bellowing, the bull kicked and bucked, yet still Enkidu held on with all his strength. Now, Gilgamesh, too, leapt down besides them, gleaming sword in hand.

"Quickly!" cried Enkidu, as the bull lashed him with its rope-thick tail. "Here is our chance to make our names. Strike between its neck and its horns."

With a flash of metal and a ferocious roar, Gilgamesh thrust his sword down. Stunned and foaming at the mouth, the blood-soaked bull staggered and swayed, before crashing, dead, to the ground. Above the sound of the city cheering came the hateful howl of the spurned goddess Ishtar, cursing the bull-killers and plunging Uruk into long years of drought.

Unmoved by her cry, Gilgamesh stood by the body of the bull, admiring its huge horns plated with lapis-lazuli. Quickly, he ordered the royal armorer to remove them. Then, he filled them with oil and offered them first to the gods.

Gilgamesh and the Bull

"From this day on, they will hang in my palace," he said, "to remind me of this moment. For I have slain the Bull of Heaven and taken my rightful place among the heroes."

That evening, a magnificent feast was held in the palace, with celebrations lasting long into the night. And still, Ishtar stood on the parapet, wailing, plotting her revenge. That night, when sleep finally came to Enkidu, he was plagued by dreadful nightmares from which he could not wake. In them, the gods took counsel and decreed that as punishment for killing the Bull of Heaven either Gilgamesh or Enkidu must die. Many times Enkidu tried to speak or raise his arms in protest, but in his dreams he could not be heard. In the days that followed, as Gilgamesh looked on, powerless to help, Enkidu was struck down by a fever so fierce that sweat poured from his body and dagger-sharp pain split his throbbing skull. He died with Gilgamesh, his dearest friend, distraught and weeping by his side.

Gilgamesh mourned his friend for days and weeks and, in grief, tore his clothes and hair. Having seen death, he feared his own, and he vowed to leave Uruk to find the secret of everlasting life. For this, he must seek out Utnapishtim, the only human to have ever been granted immortality by the gods. The journey to find him was long and terrible, but finally, Gilgamesh crossed the Waters of Death and found an old man—older than time itself.

"Great Utnapishtim," said Gilgamesh, "I have traveled far through fire and frost, and I have battled demons, to find you. Tell me the secret to eternal life, I beg you. I do not want to die—I cannot."

Slowly, wise Utnapishtim shook his head.

"You are a mighty king, Gilgamesh," he said, "but even mighty kings must die one day. The gods do not want you to live forever—that is not their way. You must make the most of the time you have, however long, or short, that may be. I cannot grant your wish, my son, though I will tell you a secret. Beneath the sea grows a plant armed with sharp-tipped thorns. If you can find it, it has the power to make men young again."

Gilgamesh set off without delay, carried on a rushing current of water far out into the sea. There, he dove down, deeper and deeper, to the seabed, rocks tied around his ankles to keep him from being swept away. As he clung to the rocks, he spied the magical plant—a tangle of green leaves and thorns. He grasped it, urgently, and rose to the surface before his chest burst for want of air.

Now the time had come for Gilgamesh to return to drought-struck Uruk and take his rightful place as king. His people were suffering, for he had abandoned them in their hour of need. And so he began his long journey. On the way, travel-weary, he spotted a pool of cool water and, placing the plant carefully down, decided to bathe. As he dreamt sweet dreams of home, a fork-tongued snake crept out of a rock crevice and devoured the plant so that not a trace remained. Despairing, Gilgamesh wept. Had his journey been for nothing, after all? Had all his best efforts truly brought no reward?

But when Gilgamesh reached Uruk and sighted the familiar roofs and houses of his beloved city, he finally realized the truth of wise old Utnapishtim's words. From this day forward, he would live his life better, rule better, and, in memory of his dearest friend, Enkidu, make the most of the time he had on Earth, however long or short it may be.

SIRIUS

The Dog in Heaven

A TALE FROM INDIA

The brightest star in the night sky is Sirius, the Dog Star. It is the star that marked the flooding of the River Nile in Ancient Egypt each year and the hottest dog days of summer in Ancient Greece. In ancient India it was known as Svana, a dog sent by the gods to test the kindness of a king.

★ ★ ★

For many years, King Yudhisthira ruled his kingdom wisely and well. Skilled in his duties as a king, he was loved by his people for his goodness and humility. But long years of war had taken their toll. The king felt worn and old, and his attachment to this life was no longer great.

His four younger brothers felt the same, and together, they decided that the time had come to give up their worldly life and make their way to heaven, high up among the snow-capped Himalayan Mountains. Yudhisthira left his throne to his grandson, and a grand and glittering coronation was held to mark the occasion. Once they had said their farewells, the time came for the brothers to leave the kingdom. Barefoot and dressed in humble robes of white, they set off on their last and greatest journey.

By the time they reached the mountains a small brown dog had joined them, trotting at their heels. No one knew where it had come from, but it followed, faithfully, never leaving Yudhisthira's side. The brothers named it "Svana" and returned its devotion tenfold.

As they climbed higher, the harder it became. For the slopes were steep, the air was thin, and the brothers were old and their bodies weak. One by one, they fell by the wayside and died, until only Yudhisthira was left. Gathering his strength, he trudged on, higher and higher into the peaks, alone now except for his loyal brown dog.

Finally, the two companions reached the roof of the world, and what he saw took Yudhisthira's breath away. All around lay snowy summits and sun-struck ridges. Far below, rushing rivers in shadowy valleys sparkled in the sunlight. Into this snow-bright landscape there rode a figure, shining with an even more brilliant light. It was Lord Indra, King of Heaven, in a splendid chariot that dazzled with diamonds and pearls.

"Good Yudhisthira," he called, "what has taken you so long? I have been waiting for you to arrive."

"Forgive me, my Lord," replied Yudhisthira. "I am on my way, but I am old and slow."

"Come," said Indra. "Climb into my chariot. I shall take you to heaven myself."

Yudhisthira felt nothing but relief—it had been a long and difficult journey, and he was tired. As he began to climb in, the little dog jumped up beside him.

"No, not the dog," said Indra. "There is no room for a dog in heaven."

The Dog in Heaven

"Then there is no room for me either," said Yudhisthira, sadly. "This dog has been my faithful companion, while everyone else was lost. I will not abandon him."

He made to get down from the chariot, but as he looked around to call for Svana, the dog was nowhere to be seen.

"That little dog was your father, Lord Dharma," said Indra, smiling at the puzzled king. "He was sent to test your kindness, and you have passed with flying colors. Goodness lies in the humblest of actions, as well as the mightiest."

So, the king climbed aboard Lord Indra's chariot and sped off through the skies to heaven. And Svana, his faithful dog, was honored with a place high among the stars.

CYGNUS AND THE MILKY WAY

The Bridge of Magpies

A TALE FROM CHINA

On either side of the Milky Way, separated by a shimmering river of stars, shine Vega and Altair, two of the brightest beacons in the sky. Destined only to meet once a year, across a magpie bridge, theirs is a tragic story of star-crossed and undying love.

Many years ago, there were two brothers who quarreled. The older brother drove the younger out of the house, leaving him to wander the land. Homeless and hungry, the boy was taken in by a kind farmer, who put him in charge of looking after his old ox. From that moment on, the boy and the ox became the closest of companions. Every day, they roamed the hills, and every night, they slept on the cowshed straw.

Years passed by, until, one day, to the boy's surprise, the ox turned his head towards him and spoke in a deep, lowing voice.

"My friend," he rumbled, "you have looked after me faithfully, but I am

old and my time on Earth is
nearly done. Soon, I must return to the
heavens and take my rightful place among the stars, but before I go, I wish to see
you married."

Thrown into confusion, the boy did not know how to reply. He did not know
any girls at all, let alone any who might marry him.

"Listen carefully," the star-born ox continued. "I will tell you what you must
do. Today is the seventh day of the seventh month—the only day on which
the worlds of the gods and humans meet. Tonight, the seven weaving girls
of heaven will descend to Earth to swim in the river. The seventh daughter
of the skies wears robes of red. You must go down to the riverside and steal
her robes. Then she will marry you, mark my words. You must go, before it's
too late."

The boy was too surprised to speak, so did what the old ox told him and

made his way, that very

evening, to the riverbank.

Hiding behind a tree, he saw, sure enough, the weaving girls, splashing in the water. Just as the ox had instructed, he crept forward and stole the red robes of the seventh weaving girl. The evening drew on, and soon it was time for the girls to return to heaven and their duties, weaving colorful clouds for the sky. But the seventh daughter could not find her robes, and the others left without her. Seeing her dismay at being left behind, the boy stepped out from behind the tree.

"Most beautiful daughter of the skies," he stuttered. "I will return your robes if you will agree to marry me."

Angry, the girl refused at first, but she saw how kind and faithful the boy was, and finally, she agreed to become his wife. So, while her sisters returned to the skies, she remained with her husband on Earth. The two loved each other very much, and when their two children were born, their happiness seemed complete. Sadly, it was not set to last. The Queen of Heaven was furious to discover that her youngest daughter was missing. She scanned the Earth until, finally, she found her.

"It is forbidden," she shrieked, "for a goddess to marry a human! I will not allow this." As she screamed, thunder split the sky apart.

In her rage, she sent her guards to Earth with a message for her daughter. She must return to the skies, without delay, to take up her duties, or face the death of her earthly family. Broken-hearted, the girl had no choice—she had to obey her mother. Weeping an ocean of tears, she said goodbye to her husband and children, and let the guards lead her away.

The cowherd acted quickly. He put his son and daughter into two baskets then climbed on to his faithful ox's back. The ox flew high up into the heavens and swept them to the palace of the Queen of Heaven, where the cowherd fell to his knees before her jade-jeweled throne.

"Majesty, I beg you," he pleaded, pitifully, "let me see my wife. We are married and are happy. Do not let us be apart."

With a face as fierce as the thunder she had created, the Queen of Heaven said nothing but, silently, reached up to her hair and pulled out a shining silver hairpin. With one swift move, she cast it across the heavens so that it tore a great silver river of stars. On one side of the river she placed her grieving daughter; on the other, the cowherd, destined to be, forever, apart. Only once every year, on the seventh day of the seventh lunar month, does the hard-hearted Queen of Heaven show mercy. On that day, every fortune-bringing magpie on Earth flies to heaven to build a magical bridge across the Silver River so that the Cowherd and the Weaving Girl can reunite once more.

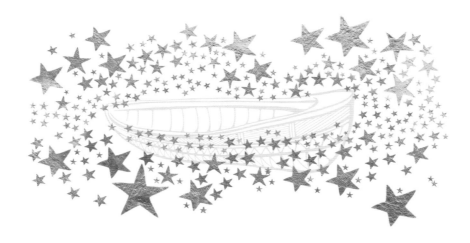

THE MILKY WAY
The Canoe of Stars
A MAORI TALE

Sprinkled across the night, a scattering of stardust forms a brilliant band of light. Within it, there are countless billions of stars, but look carefully and you may also see the shape of a canoe, sailing peacefully through the sky-ocean.

Long, long ago, there were no stars in the sky at night. The darkness was so deep that people could not move about without bumping into things. The only beings that could find their way in the gloom were the Taniwha, watchful guardian spirits of nature. They spent their days hiding in caves and pools, and their nights lurking in the shadows, ensnaring prey, even humans, to eat.

Among the people, there lived a brave warrior called Tama-rereti. One warm, bright morning, he decided to go fishing in the lake near his home. He loaded up his canoe with lines and bait and, in no time at all, had reached his favorite fishing place. After a few hours, his baskets filled with fish, he made to head for home. But the wind had dropped to a whisper and Tama-rereti began

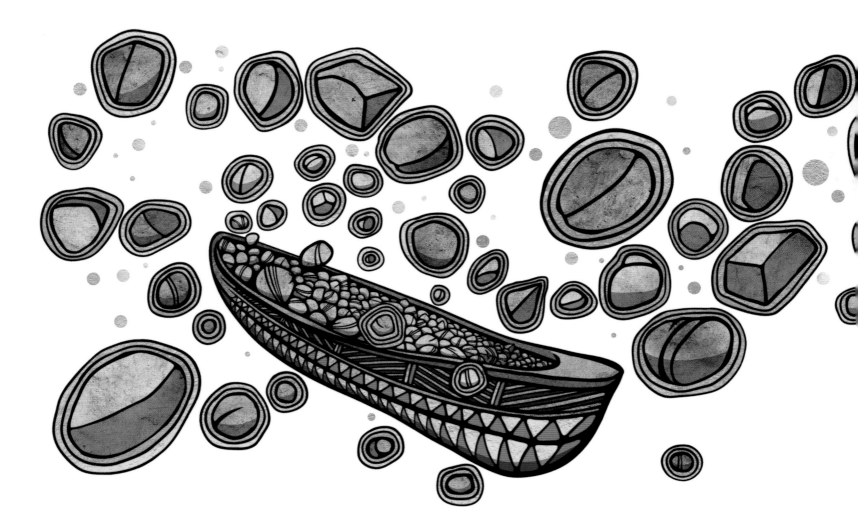

to feel weary. He lay down in the bottom of his canoe and soon nodded off to sleep with the sound of the waves gently lapping.

Some time later, Tama-rereti woke up with a start. He had slept soundly for hours. While he slumbered, his canoe had drifted quietly on the breeze until it had reached the far end of the lake. By now, he was a long way from home, and the day was growing late. He would not be able to get back before dusk fell, and after dusk, the Taniwha would be on the prowl! Tama-rereti would need to gather his strength, and realizing that his belly was empty, he dragged his canoe onto the nearby beach and left it resting upon the smooth silver pebbles. There, he lit a fire and cooked a fish. All the while, his eye was caught by the glint and gleam of the pebbles, caught in the fire's dancing flames.

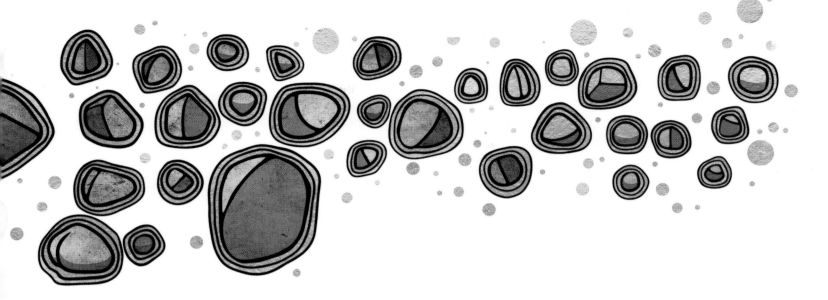

By now, night was falling fast. Tama-rereti knew he must devise a plan—and quickly. Then he had an idea. Loading his canoe with as many shimmering pebbles as it could hold, he pushed off from the shore. "Instead of going home," he said to himself, "I shall sail along the great river that empties into heaven."

Just as the Sun slipped beneath the horizon and a blanket of darkness descended on the Earth, Tama-rereti steered his canoe upwards, to the river in the sky. As he sailed along, he took handfuls of pebbles and scattered them in their thousands, in all directions, to become the stars. Now, he could see well enough by this starry torchlight to find his way home before dawn.

When Tama-rereti finally reached his house, he found Ranginui, the sky god, waiting for him. Brave warrior though he was, Tama-rereti was afraid that Ranginui had come to scold him for littering the sky. But the great god was happy to see the sky so bright with light.

"Thanks to your quick-thinking, not only is the land safer, the night sky is more beautiful than before," he said. "So that people may always remember what you have done, your canoe will be placed, for eternity, among the stars." And there it remains, to this day, sailing peacefully through the night.

Hina and the Shark

A TONGAN TALE

High above the Pacific, an empty canoe weaves its graceful way across the ocean in the sky, accompanied by a glittering line of fish. Its passengers lie deep beneath the sea, tossed and turned by the waves on a coral reef.

On the islands of Tonga, a story is told of a beautiful girl from a high-born family and a shark that she loved and lost. The girl's name was Hina, and she lived long ago, in a fine house, with her three brothers. Her parents doted on their only daughter and made sure that she had everything her heart could desire.

One day, the boys and their father went out fishing in their canoe and caught a baby shark on the reef. In this part of the world, sharks were feared and revered in equal measure, for they were thought to be gifts from the gods.

"Do not kill it!" shouted the father, as his son raised his spear to strike. "We will give it to Hina as a pet."

As close to the shore as they dared, they blocked off the channels to create

Hina and the Shark

a pool in the reef where the shark could swim and Hina could come to feed it. Day after day, Hina talked and played with her new companion, stroking its gray head as it swam by. And, day after day, the shark grew bigger, as Hina grew ever fonder of it.

Then, one evening, the sky went dark, the wind whipped up, and a violent storm unleashed its fury over Hina's island, sending the people running for safety. Savage waves crashed on to the seashore, smashing the reef apart, and the shark was lost. Some say that it was swept out to sea; others that it took its chance to be free, at last.

Hina's grief knew no bounds. For days, she wept bitterly. In despair, she went to her parents and begged them to paddle out in their canoe to search for her beloved pet. So, the three—mother, father, and daughter—set sail into the open waters, which were only now beginning to calm. Far and wide, high and low, they searched, while Hina called. Finally, to Hina's delight, a fin suddenly emerged from the deep. There was no doubt to whom it belonged—Hina recognized her shark at once.

"Come back with me," she called. "We will build another pool for you."

But the shark had tasted freedom, swimming far and free across the open sea, and it did not want to return. Hina could not bear to be parted from her friend again, so she jumped over the edge of the boat to become part of the rocky reef where sharks could hide in times of churning storms. Her doting parents followed, while their canoe rose up in the heavens to become the stars of Alotulu, "three in a boat," known to some as the belt of Orion.

PLEIADES

The Seven Sisters

AN AUSTRALIAN ABORIGINAL TALE

The seven bright stars of the Pleiades shine like a beacon, burning in the dark. Among the Aboriginal people of Australia, they were once seven earthly sisters, transformed into beings of light.

Once, in the Dreamtime, when the spirits roamed the Earth, there lived seven sisters, called the Karatgurk. Together, they shared a great secret. Each sister carried a burning coal on the end of a digging stick, which they used to make fire. They guarded their fire-coals closely and told no one of their secret, though many, both human and animal, were deadly jealous of their knowledge. For not only could they use fire to keep warm, but they also used it to cook the yams that they dug out of the ground each morning.

One day, Crow, sly old trickster, sneaked up close and stole a cooked yam from the sisters. It was tastier than anything he had ever eaten before. He begged the sisters, again, to share their knowledge of fire, but they refused and shooed

The Seven Sisters

him away. In a rage, Crow hopped from leg to leg and back again, squawking harshly, and vowed, there and then, to steal the secret by trickery. So, cunning Crow caught some snakes in his sharp black beak and hid them inside an anthill. He called to the sisters to show off his discovery. "Look what I've found," he cawed, boastfully. "The biggest, juiciest honey ants you'll ever taste. They're far more delicious than yams any day, and there are lots of them over here."

The sisters picked up their sticks and began digging, for honey ants were their favorite food. But, as they dug, the snakes slithered out, biting and hissing. Shrieking, the sisters beat the snakes back so hard that the red-hot coals flew off the ends of their digging sticks. Crow's trick had worked! Quickly, he gathered up the coals and hid them in a kangaroo-skin bag. When the sisters realized, horrified, what had happened, they gave chase, but fire-thieving Crow simply flapped his wings and flew to the top of a tall tree, out of reach.

Eaglehawk, who had seen all of this, called to Crow. "Give me some of your coals, Brother Crow," he said, "so that I can cook this opossum."

"Give the opossum to me, Brother Eaglehawk," replied Crow. "I shall cook it for you instead."

But the secret was out now, and soon a huge crowd of animals had collected around Crow's tree, demanding that he share the fire. Louder and louder grew the noise, startling Crow so that he flung some of the burning coals at the crowd. Hissing and crackling, fire took hold, racing across the bush. Crow's feathers were burned as black as soot—as they are to this day. Still the fire roared, threatening to destroy the land, until the rains came and halted its spread. Meanwhile, their secret gone for good, the Karatgurk sisters were swept up into the sky, where their still-glowing digging sticks became seven bright-burning stars.

THE SUN

The Emu Egg and the Sun

AN AUSTRALIAN ABORIGINAL TALE

A very long time ago, before there were people on Earth, there were animals and birds, much bigger than those that roam today. There was no Sun shining in the sky above, only the Moon and the stars.

One day, a terrible commotion broke out on the great plain below. Dinewan the emu and Brolga the crane fought and quarreled, squawking and shrieking, while tempers frayed and feathers flew. In her rage, Brolga ran over to Dinewan's nest in a hollowed-out scrape on the ground and seized one of the huge eggs in her beak. Then she hurled the egg, with all of her might, into the sky. Tossed high into the heavens, the egg landed on a huge pile of firewood and cracked open, spilling its yellow yolk and causing the wood to burst into flames. Below, the world was lit up by the blaze, and the animals that lived in the half-light were dazzled by its fiery glow. And so, the Sun was born.

The cloud man, Ngoudenout, saw how beautiful the Earth looked when the sky-fire burned. "I will make a fire every day," he said, "so the day will never

92

grow dark again."

At night, while the fire burned out, he set off into the forest and collected wood to build a pile. When the heap was high enough, he sent out the Morning Star to warn those on Earth that the fire was soon to be lit, bringing the rosy pinks of dawn. But though the Morning Star shone brightly, it was not enough. Those who slept did not see it and did not wake to see the day arrive. Instead, the spirits decided they should find a noise loud enough to wake those still sleeping and herald each new day. For a long time, they debated over what noise would be the best. Then, one morning, they heard the laughter of Kookaburra, ringing through the air.

"This is exactly the noise we need," they agreed. "It will wake even the deepest sleeper."

And so they instructed Kookaburra that every morning, as the Morning Star faded, he must laugh his loudest laugh. If he did not, the sun-fire would go out, plunging the Earth into half-light once more. Proud Kookaburra did not fail, and to this day he laughs at his loudest in the hour before dawn.

"Goo goor gaga! Goo goor gaga!" he sings, saving the Sun for the world.

And, each day, Ngoudenout still makes his fire. Though it does not throw out much heat at first, by noon its heat is fiercer, as the wood fully catches fire. After that, it slowly dies down, until by evening its light is spent and night falls over the Earth. Then, Ngoudenout covers the glowing embers with clouds, ready to light the fire the following day.

THE MILKY WAY

Emu in the Sky

AN AUSTRALIAN ABORIGINAL TALE

Look towards the Southern Cross and you may spot the shape of an emu striding, long-legged, through the skies. The dark cloud between the stars is the emu's head. Its neck, body, and legs are formed from dust trails, stretching across the river of stars.

In the Dreamtime, countless years ago, a great wind whipped up and Emu was blown on the breeze high up into the sky. For time unknown, she wandered, lost in the vast expanse of space, looking for somewhere to rest. The first place she found was in the gentle, hollow curve of the crescent Moon, but as time passed, the Moon grew fat and pushed her out of her lunar nest.

Next, Emu made her way to the camp of the stars and asked if she could live with them. To decide Emu's fate, the stars called a meeting. They discussed and they deliberated, and finally, they all agreed that Emu could stay, on one condition—she must help them with their work of holding up the sky, for the burden was heavy on them.

Now, Emu had no way of getting back to Earth. She had traveled up to heaven on a breeze, but she could not fly, so she could not get down again. She accepted the stars' offer—she had no choice in the matter, after all. Emu would help the stars to hold up the sky in return for a place to rest. So, in the part of the sky where the stars were the thickest and the load fairly shared, the stars shuffled and shoved and moved aside just enough to allow Emu a dark space for a camp.

There, Emu remains to this day. Sometimes, though, the stars like to play tricks and test Emu's strength. They move farther apart, then farther still, so that Emu must take more of the load on her back. If you listen, you can hear her groaning and grumbling in the rumbling thunder. And, every now and then, Emu grows weary and lets the sky fall a little, sending stars shooting downwards towards the Earth.